Disney's
SIMBA
THE
FORTUNE TELLER

D0108742

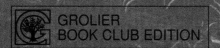

GROLIER
BOOK CLUB EDITION

ISBN: 0-7172-8832-3

Manufactured in the United States of America.
A B C D   1 2 3 4

It was a hot day in the African jungle. Simba and his two friends, Timon and Pumbaa, lounged lazily beneath a shady tree.

"Let's do something," Simba said.

"Let's not and say we did," answered Timon.

"Yeah," agreed Pumbaa. "It's too hot to do anything."

"But I'm bored!" said Simba.

"Okay, chairman of the bored," Timon said, "tell us a story."

"A story?"
Simba thought long and hard.
He could not think of a story,
but he did think of the best
storyteller he knew—Rafiki.

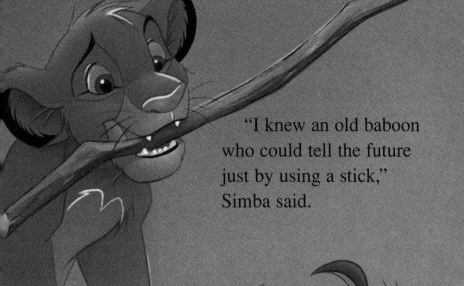

"I knew an old baboon who could tell the future just by using a stick," Simba said.

"A stick?" said Timon. "What, he couldn't afford a crystal ball?"

"Show us how he did it," Pumbaa said.

Simba drew a circle in the dirt. Then he waved the stick over it.

"Asante sana, squashed banana!"

"Put your pawprint in the circle," Simba told Timon.

"Okay, I'll play along," Timon said. "Read my future, oh, great Simbini."

Timon placed his paw in the circle. Then Simba closed his eyes and waved his stick.

"Well, what does the stick say?"
Pumbaa asked impatiently.

"Timon will face grave danger in
the near future," Simba announced.

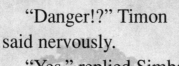

"Danger!?" Timon said nervously.

"Yes," replied Simba, "but you will show great bravery."

"You've never been brave before, Timon," Pumbaa said. "Are you scared?"

"Scared? Me?" Timon answered. "The only danger I face is standing downwind of a warthog. No offense, pal."

"My turn!" Pumbaa said.

Pumbaa put his hoof in the circle.

"Pumbaa will meet someone very special and very pretty," Simba predicted.

"That's not fair," moaned Timon.
"I get danger and he gets *romance?*
I thought you were a fortune teller,
not a *misfortune* teller."
Pumbaa tried to cheer Timon up.
"Come on, let's go rustle up some
grubs," he said.
"No, thanks," Timon said sadly.
"Oh, come on, Timon," Simba said.
"It was just a game. I'm not a fortune teller."

Just then
the boys were
joined by their
good friends
the monkeys.

"Hello!" the monkeys cried. "Do you want to play a game with us?"

"Yes!" Pumbaa said. "I love games!"

"I do, too!" added Simba. "Do you want to play, Timon?"

"No," Timon said.

"Timon, you always say there's nothing more fun than monkeying around," Simba told him.

"It's too risky," Timon said.

"Are you sure?" asked Pumbaa.

"Sure I'm sure, lover-boy," Timon answered. "You and the fortune teller go without me."

So Simba joined the monkeys for
a game of "catch."

"Ready?" the monkeys asked.

"Ready!" Simba cried.

Then the monkeys shot Simba
straight up into the air!

"WHEEEE!" Simba squealed.

"HA-KU-NA MA-TA-TA!"
they all shouted.
Timon jumped
to his feet.

"That does it!" he cried. "No one
hakunas without *this* matata!"

Timon decided to join the fun! He
hopped on the monkeys' feet and they
threw him high into the sky!

"WHEEE!"
Timon cried.

Then Timon started to fall…
"WHEE…"
…right into a hole!
"…uh, oh."

CRASH!

Everybody gathered around the hole.

"Timon!" Pumbaa yelled "Are you all right?"

"No, I'm not all right! I'm six feet underground!"

"Don't worry," Simba said, "we'll get you out. There's no danger."

"Uh…well… actually, there is *one* danger," Pumbaa said.

"What's that?" Simba asked.

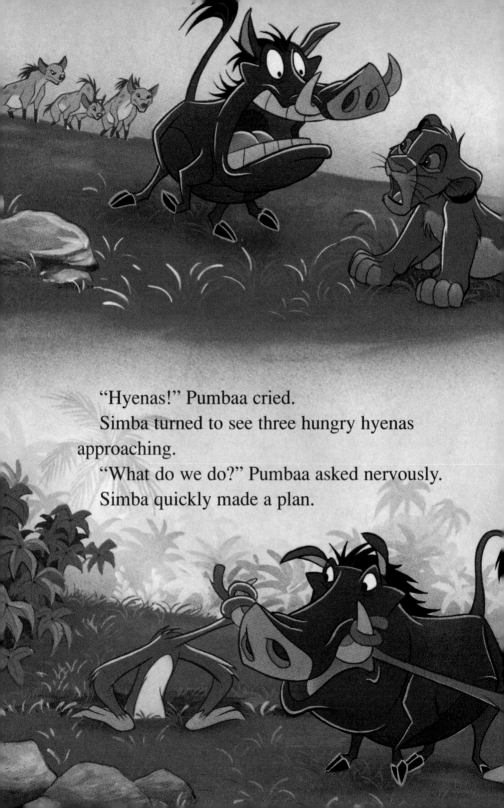

"Hyenas!" Pumbaa cried.

Simba turned to see three hungry hyenas approaching.

"What do we do?" Pumbaa asked nervously.

Simba quickly made a plan.

"Come on, everybody," Simba said, "let's make a monkey ladder!"

So Simba, Pumbaa, and the monkeys all held on to each other, reached down, and pulled Timon up.

"Thanks, kid," Timon said to Simba.
"Looks like your prediction came true!
Lucky for me the danger is over."
"It's not over yet,"
Simba cried. "Climb!"

Everybody climbed the nearest tree. Even Pumbaa
managed with a little help from his friend.

Timon clung to a branch.

"You were still wrong about the bravery part,"
he said to Simba. "I'm a coward and proud of it."

The hyenas slowly approached the tree.

"Hmm… smell that, boys?"
said the first hyena.

"Yeah," said the second hyena.
"It smells like dinner!"

"But where is it?" asked the first hyena.

"SSHHH!" Pumbaa whispered. "If we
stay quiet, maybe they'll go away."

No one in the tree made a sound. It looked as if the hyenas *would* just walk away.

Then suddenly…

CRACK!

The branch holding Pumbaa broke!

The warthog fell to the ground with a great big PLOP!

Pumbaa tried to hide in a bush, but he stuck out—a lot!

"Look!" the first hyena cried. "Supper!"

The hyenas approached Pumbaa, ready to attack, when suddenly Timon swung past them!

"Hey, doggies!" he yelled to the hyenas, "Can you mangy mutts catch a meerkat?"

The hyenas chased Timon, but they didn't look
where they were going. They fell right into the hole!
"Thanks for playing
our game," Timon shouted.
"Drop in again!"

"So, compliment me," Timon said to his friends.
"You were incredibly brave!" cried Pumbaa.
"Fantastically brave!" added Simba.
"Yes, I was, wasn't I?" said Timon.
The monkeys cheered.

Simba heard the hyenas yelping and knew
that sooner or later they would climb out of the
hole. So Simba, Pumbaa, and Timon said
good-bye to their friends.

"See, Simba?
You really *are* a
fortune teller!"
Pumbaa said as
they walked away.

The three friends went down to the river to cool off. On the shore, Pumbaa saw a very pretty hippopotamus. He smiled at her.

"Looks as though your other prediction is about to come true, too," Timon said to Simba.

Pumbaa went to talk to the hippo,
but her mother blocked him.
"My daughter doesn't speak to
smelly warthogs," she said.
Pumbaa was sad.

"Ouch!" Timon said.
"Poor Pumbaa!"
"Maybe I'm not a
fortune teller, after all,"
Simba said.

Pumbaa felt very downhearted.
"What can we do?" Simba asked Timon.
"We give Pumbaa the one thing that always makes him happy," Timon answered. "FOOD!"

Timon and Simba quickly gathered all
the slugs, grubs, and bugs they could find.

"I can make a sauce from these berries,"
Simba said.

"Yum! It'll be great with this nice big
caterpillar," Timon answered.

Simba looked over at his friend.

"Er, Timon that is not a caterpillar," Simba said.

"You can say that again!" Timon answered.

"It feels heavy enough to be a…"

"Snake!" cried Simba.

"Yeah," Timon said turning around.
"It feels heavy enough
to be a snake."
HISSSS!
"SNAKE!"
Timon yelled in horror.

Timon jumped
on Simba's back.
"Run!" he yelled.
HISSSS!

The snake tried to chase
them, but they were too fast
and managed to get away.

"Why didn't you use your amazing powers to predict that snake?" Timon asked Simba.

"I told you I wasn't a fortune teller" Simba replied.

Just then, they realized Pumbaa wasn't with them!

Then their friend jumped out of the bushes.

"Hi, guys!" he said, smiling.

"There you are!" Timon said. "We've got a special treat for you, buddy."

"Yeah," Simba added. "Do you want some bugs?"

"No," Pumbaa replied.

"WHAT!?" Timon and Simba cried in shock. "Why?"

Suddenly a pretty female warthog appeared.

"Because I want to give them to my new friend, Pika," said Pumbaa.

"Hello, boys," Pika said. "Do you have any more bugs for Pumbaa?" she asked.

Timon looked at Simba.

"You may be the fortune teller, kid,"
Timon joked, "but I predict that with two
hungry warthogs, we're going to need a lot
more food around here!"